Dawn Changes Everything

Karim Benammar

PLETHORA

Author: Karim Benammar

Author photograph: François Luxembourg

Cover photograph by the author: Madeira.

ISBN: 9789493375000

See the sun rise over her skin

Don't change it

See the sunrise over her skin

Dawn changes everything

U2, *Heartland*

Contents

1. Waking 1
2. Waves 3
3. Monsoon Rains 5
4. Woman Coming Out of the Bath 9
5. Chopin in New Orleans 11
6. The Way of Tea 13
7. Japanese Child 15
8. Words 17
9. The Hood of the Saab 19
10. Silence and the Buddha 21
11. Landing 23
12. Dancing 25
13. Connections 27
14. Seashore 29
15. Brasserie 31
16. Downriver 33

17. Surrender 35

18. Traces 37

19. Reflections 39

20. Ballroom 41

21. Whirling 43

22. Mirrors 45

23. Boardroom 47

24. Perfect Day 49

25. Slow song 51

26. Intermezzo 53

27. Exile 55

28. Perpetuum Immobile 57

29. Shadows 59

30. Instant 61

31. Clouds 63

32. Levity 65

33. I Am Legion 67

34. Survivor's Pride 71

35. The Last One Before the Final One 73

1
Waking

This breast, this nipple: its presence, carnal, pores and dark skin, immediately *here*. It exists as reflected patterns of light coming from the open window, the play of shapes on the curved flesh in league with the breeze stirring the curtains. Over your shoulder, beyond that breast, out of focus, an indeterminate beyond. The lightness of morning, the becoming-things of objects, the way the light suffuses the impermanence of things, their barely controlled volatility - reality itself floats like particles of dust. Things slowly congeal, coalesce into solidity, into matter, and gradually become irrevocably present, *here*.

The morning itself began with your words, started with your whispers overlaying the murmurs of the day. I am still pressed against you, my curled-up shape cradling yours, covering your back with my weight, protectively. It is not the world that is massive, heavy, inexorable, you said. It is in my body itself that I find the sense and meaning of weight. My body is always weighed down, touches the world in all these places, my sensual self hostage to gravity. Objects around me, including the earth I walk on, are in a way as boundless and light as the sky itself. When I wake, the world around me slowly reconstitutes itself, objects acquire their characteristic heaviness. For a while, they are at the mercy of the morning light, they are not yet things.

2

Waves

These feelings are like riding waves of pleasure, she says, like windsurfing, skidding over the top, a flat stone ricocheting over the water, staccato flight over crests, a rhythm born out of the hollow clack-clack-clack of the board hitting walls of water, in tune with the swoosh of the silage. The board's nose rises out of the water, hangs in the air, propelled above the waves, aiming at the sun, swallowing up the space in front of it, poised for flight. Of course, I hang in there, the weight of my body against the wind, the sail blowing me away, balanced against the gusts, following the board's nose wherever it will take me.

That is how I feel these days, skidding over the waves of the world around me, as I am walking down the street, pocketing my change from the newspaper man. There are days I can only think in waves, only in terms of change and flow, tops and troughs, crests and valleys. There are only currents animating the living things in the world, their alternating positions elegantly and continuously traded.

What is around me no longer seems composed of immutable objects, of heavy solids ruled by gravitational pull, or by the distinct order they embody. Everything dances, wavers, the foliage of the trees pulsates: currents run through everything. People too are traversed by this current, guided by it, no longer individuals but flows and ripples in a sea of bodies.

3
Monsoon Rains

Do you remember the heavy rains, she asks, when the laden sky empties itself into mountains and trees, into springs and rivers - the heavy monsoon rain in the late afternoon, streaks of rain illuminated by the fading light? It is the sound of that rain, a blanket of clattering raindrops, the distinctive sound of droplets hitting leaves, a corrugated iron roof, a puddle, all these discrete droplets in their ultimate swansong before crashing out of their ephemeral existence.

This blanket cover of sound, this multitude of drops, is joined by the growling, threatening bass of thunder, and by the gurgling sound of water seeping across the ground, along the broad cover of the leaves, overflowing leaking gutters. In this rain all these sounds can be distinguished if you cup your ear - if you listen, really, attentively.

Suddenly the rain increases in intensity, as if all this water were hurled to earth by an angry, annoyed God, thrown with terrifying strength, the intensity of sound also rising, drops of rain now in a mad race to annihilate themselves, jets of water bouncing off all surfaces, ricocheting back into the air, colliding with the downpour, tracing arabesques in the air, tiny fountains springing up. You feel you are that multitude of droplets, tiny thoughts clattering and your senses welling up, resonating briefly inside before vanishing. Sheltered from the cloudburst, you feel secure, protected, at the same time witness and exempt.

The cleansing rain brings out the smell of plants, flowers, tree bark, and the hidden, covered smell of the dusty ground; the air, purified, fills with a heady fragrance which fills your lungs and soul. The earth re-emerges as from a slumber, the fragrant garden discloses itself, proudly fills the air - mists of an olfactory Eden - Ah, to smell the world.

It is a peculiar blend of nostalgia and relief, the dying day slowly buried in its shadows, foliage taking on darkened hues, the silhouettes of tall trees, sharp and distinct against pale skies, all of this suffused by a liberating celestial downpour, the earth itself washed and rejuvenated, the lingering dust of the day cleared, rubbed out, scrubbed.

The heart too is full - this time invites memories, voices, and images of lost scenes in your life, which return and, unbidden, come to the fore. Faraway friends and erstwhile lovers - they too had their time, and those times have disappeared, swallowed up and erased by an evening shower such as this. It is as if all your fleeting joys and loves, your attachments and desires are also fading with the light, but slowly, peacefully, surrendering themselves without much of a struggle.

Now that shadows and hues have deepened still, the first freshness of the night imposes itself, and this particular nostalgia fills you to the core, weighs on you. To escape these accumulated memories, I need to be held, cuddled, enclosed - and you held me, protective, gazing over my shoulder, your nose and ears and mouth so close to mine, your quiet breathing mingling with the air, your nostrils, like mine, aflutter, your ears too registering every drop of this blanket sound. But it is your warmth, the cradle of your lap, your hands upon mine, our fingers complicitously intertwined, it is feeling you so close, so present, here, that chases the dark shadows from the skies and my heart.

Protected from the rain, I am protected from its gloomy spell, its enchanted power to re-awaken and summon memories. You, no less than the rain, than the depth of the dark blue skies, the graceful branches of the tall trees, and the incessant pit-pat of the thundering rain, belong here, belong next to me, with me. Your inaudible, perhaps unspoken whispers accompany the clatter of raindrops; your musk intermingles with the shamelessly fragrant flowers, your carnal presence soothing. Were you not completely mine, then, in the downpour, was I not completely yours, in the heavy shadows, were we not both in the world, of the world, world?

As every lingering moment passes, this enchantment too fades into the darkness of the encroaching night, and the shadows have now taken over, covering up the last glimmering leaves. The rain too has stopped, drowned the vestiges of the day and ushered in the night. We sigh, contented, stretch, and head into the bright lights of the evening, to exorcise the dark shadows of the night, to placate the ghosts of unearthed memories. Having religiously buried the day, and taken leave of the sun pursuing its mad incandescent course across the surface of the globe, elsewhere.

Do you remember the monsoon rains?

4

Woman Coming Out of the Bath

I am a child of the oceans, she confides, of freezing depths and warm lagoons, my mind intoxicated by winds from the sea, traces of salt drying on my skin, a child in search of home, seeking solace in lakes, streams, showers, baths. I desire elemental fluid, waters running down my body, a chaotic multitude of patterns on my skin, I need to be submerged, enveloped, cradled and numbed by the heat of the waters.

I cannot possess your body by merely looking at it, by discovering its shapes and contours, soft curves and sharp angles, the pattern of hairs on skin, or its history of wrinkles and little scars. From every perspective, your body hides part of itself, reveals less than it conceals from view; the reality of its presence, solid, the essence of its movements, graceful, escapes even my most fervent gaze.

Of course, if I can touch, use my own body for exploration, I enter into and submit to an entirely different realm of the senses. A tiny patch of I, a surface of skin that is already dead, four fingertips pursue an itinerary of desire on that body, yours, tracing inscriptions of lust, kneading flesh, scraping lines of possession with fingernails. But by teasing, exposing the surface of your body, its alterity is revealed, its obeisance to its own laws, passions, and convulsions, even when I draw it into the space of my desire.

The skin of this other body, yours, shines in its wetness; beads of moisture decorate your forehead, drops escape from long black hair glued in strands to your back. The water flows along your surfaces, delineating and polishing its curves like it would the bed of a stream, confirming the geography of your body, giving it relief. The stream branches out into rivulets, randomly crisscrossing patterns of hair on your body, smoothing its design into streaks, enveloping every pore.

The water splashes everywhere; it follows the contours of your body into its most hidden places, tingles where the skin folds back upon itself, awakening nerves. It splashes from all sides, needles of pleasure hitting you from all directions, confusing and redrawing your awareness of surfaces and limbs, making you all arm, all thigh, all back.

The waters stir, and your body undulates, inside a shallow wave. The water streams past your legs, your slow movements creating gentle currents, softer than a caress; now you are only these legs, the rest of you melted, liquefied. Your body, water, floats in water, your body hangs, liquid, hot. Your body, at rest, is turned inside out, its sensory surfaces, numbed, spreading; its inner, heated core radiating well-being.

This is how my eyes take possession of you, this is how I caress your skin, cover your body, glide along it, dispersed in liquid paths that find their way upon you, enveloping you in my warmth, holding all of you, everywhere, inside your ears and mouth, between your toes. I am this water that cools and burns, that washes over you, I flush away dirt and tiredness, soothe your muscles; I am this water that makes you shine, resplendent, the heat that flushes your chest; I am this water that makes you the most languorous, sensual, and intoxicating of women.

And as you step out of the bath, I long to be the multitude of tiny silver droplets that glide over your skin and, spent, crash to the floor.

5

Chopin in New Orleans

I think of these Chopin notes lingering in the moist New Orleans air, and how my heart moves with every key depressed on the piano, following its mad dance, cajoling, seductive, until it builds up to produce rich cascades, waterfalls of drops of time, notes that roll over each other into the future, splashing here and there, turmoil and scales, sound that, now controlled, recaptures its melody and rests, leaving behind sparkles in the night.

I think of the smooth ride in your car in the dark, the grand houses of St. Charles passing in slow motion, and this music that envelops us both. In such moments even time slows down and rests, suspended, for a while. I think about nestling up to your shoulder, smelling your neck, your hair on my forehead, seeing only part of your face from the side, your legs entwined in mine, and about how safe I feel then.

And I think about the earth that spins madly underneath my feet as I walk, and about my own happiness at this very moment, which grows out of me to envelop these dark buildings, draws together the streetlights, this happiness that I breathe out, at this moment now large enough to encompass even the stars in this night and the lives of all the people that are in my thoughts.

6

The Way of Tea

Autumn has enveloped Kyoto in its most glorious colours; drunken Gods have painted the trees in fiery crimson red and luminescent yellows. The moist smell of temple garden moss and fallen leaves evokes the melancholy sense of *mono no aware*, the passing of cherished things, and invites a chill in the air.

The woman in kimono kneels down, and with meticulous, carefully choreographed moves, pours the scalding water from the earthen pot. A single flower in a clay vase is shadowed by strokes of ink on a calligraphy scroll. The rustling of garments and wooden sandals on straw mats, the sweetness of the leaf-shaped confection before the draught of bitter green tea. Our five senses aflutter.

Ichi go, ichi e: one encounter, one moment. Space folds in upon itself. Time rests, in silence.

The whole universe is indeed present in this secluded moment, as I feel waves of pleasure spread from your body, intensely cat-like in its crouched position, radiating outward to envelop the corners of this, now our, world. Soseki imagines a three-cornered world: the corner of common sense left out, perhaps forgotten, perhaps waylaid.

7

Japanese Child

At dusk, a Japanese child dances down the road; her laugh of childish joy, illuminated by copper sun rays, hits me with stunning immediacy. The child draws it all in, the peaceful suburb, the neatly arranged front doors and occasional shrubs, while adults are moving to and fro, occupied. She draws in every perspective, glimpsed from afar, focusing as our paths and eyes meet, as I look back over my shoulder, mesmerised. Conversely, she exudes it all, too: this quiet road exists by the grace of her happiness, of which it must be constituted, its careful arrangements having so far escaped her capricious whims, and the world still constitutes a colossal playground, stretching infinitely outward.

Her laugh, still ringing, carries with it the promise that everything can bring, when any discarded piece of plastic becomes, through child's magic, a weapon, a bridge, a treasure to be buried or hidden at home; it is witness to a time when reality is fluid, malleable, conspiratorial. This moment, as sunlight schemes with the child's laugh, when happiness manifests itself as golden joy, an interplay of light, shadows and sound, momentary yet unforgettable, inscribes itself into my soul.

8
Words

It is at the moment when you are about to speak, when words, already formed, are weighed once more, held back, queued up, as if your imagination holds them hostage a little longer, when they are mouthed silently, helplessly, your lips pursed like a mute fish, your eyebrows testimony to bearing pains, that the world is also on hold, captive, not yet fully formed, waiting.

I know you by the way your body falls forward, extends itself towards others as if to embrace them. Your eyes shine and seduce me into trusting you, into opening my world to yours. Your hands move with exaggerated, generous gestures: quick, strong, they draw in the magnificence of the plaza on which we stand, mimic its grandeur.

They cup invisible bowls as you speak of what matters, they draw arcs of disbelief at the lies of men, they cradle tender thoughts in need of conviction.

9

The Hood of the Saab

The sky inversely reflected in the hood of the Saab, ghost lights disappearing on both sides beyond the curved metal edge, thrusting forward between those lights, beckoned, invited, entranced. Balance: driving at night, the music - *Blue Moon Revisited* - taking over my feelings, carried away by a pacing bass and soft haunting voice, the lights of the stretched-out highway reflected in the hood, the powerful engine pushing the silent car closer to its destiny, towards the hugs and kisses of return. Nothing better than moving closer to friends and lovers, on the way, already engaged with their thoughts and desires, wrapped in memories of their words and sighs.

Indifferent to all this, the car glides, swallowing up time and distance before it, wheels turning, headlights scanning the smooth darkness, a few red and white beacons emerging from the bluish dark, other travellers on their way. Balance: time rests, suspended, floats on the melody, with minimal control to steer the machine. Thoughts wander, scan the past: memories well up, softly - voices of friends, landscapes, ethereal musings which linger awhile, then float away to disappear in the dark.

10

Silence and the Buddha

Speaking about silence is paradoxical. Silence at first is nothing but a reprieve, an empty measure of time, a buffer between words. Usually, a pause is not intended as a silence; silence only comes into its own as it prolongs itself, as it acquires its own gravity to outweigh sound. Then the absence of words begins to be felt keenly, as a privation, a painful lack - silence is meaning slipping away, absenting itself, withdrawing from the world.

When silence takes hold, it controls the flow of words, damming up their relentless current to establish a new norm, a competing sensitivity, a different language. Yet its hold remains precarious, for it will eventually negate itself by its own rule - a silence prolonged, carried forward, gently rubbing out and erasing the echo of voices, dims the memory of its very substance, reduces itself to a mute state without memories, when even the possibility of sound itself is forgotten. Will we still recognize sound, will hearing remain; will we not be confronted with something categorically different, then?

A Buddha statue's beatific, enlightened smile, indifferent to words, inner and outer repose: I find myself bathed in a lingering silence, as your shinning eyes are locked into mine, and time, devoid of its auditory marker, fades and dissolves between us.

11

Landing

At times I feel like a plane coming in to land, she says, suspended in the burning evening sky, wings outstretched, landing gear lowered, zeroing in on the time when the rubber will touch down on the shimmering tarmac, when, mission accomplished, the prodigal returns home, fragrant with the smells of faraway spices, laden with the memories of unspoken desires and whispered confessions.

It is in that time before confirmation, with the future already engaged, the descent about to be fulfilled, irrevocable, the cast dice in mid-air, everything given, gambled, committed, it is in that timeless stretched moment that the heart bursts its ripe fullness, that the soul itself floats, finds its rightful place in the indefinite vastness of space, resonates with an overwhelming, overflowing *now*.

The wheels hang a fraction above the runway, the plane fully horizontal, its wing flaps measuring the remaining friction, the moment of contact imminent, eddies of turbulence forming in its wake, the last sliver of time before the lightness of two hundred tonnes of steel held aloft, floating, is again transformed into a rumbling, rolling, hissing, screeching juggernaut barrelling on the ground.

Even then, with unlived time racing towards the moment of impact at the same speed as the airplane itself, with the future as fixed as the relentless pull of gravity on the mass of curved steel, with destiny and fate about to coalesce, the world glides by in slow-motion, held in the glow of a lingering present.

And at the close, anticipation stretched beyond itself, release is an elated rush of the energies of reverse engine thrust, wheels spinning, the heat of metal on metal, the violent kiss of rubber and concrete, fluids racing crisscross through tubes and pipes, power and pressure, the jolt and shiver of solid ground, muscles bracing themselves against momentum.

The steel colossus rolls on, again paced, at leisure, manoeuvred, steered, towards the final white line where it comes to rest, the hiss of its propulsion switched off.

Home.

12

Dancing

Our world does not contain the dancer, she whispers: the dancer creates the space of the world through her movements, like Shiva. The dancer is in sync with the world, attunes herself to it, falls into counter-beat phase. Space curves, receives, yields, invites her body to press against it, to fill it up, it bids it come.

The dancing body beckons outside of itself, its circles and caresses creating and annihilating space, its weight leaning on the lightness of air. The dancer spins, arms outstretched, falling into the interstices between spaces, sucked in by vortices of air. The body of the dancer becomes inside turned outside, inside flaunted as outside. Curiosity and joy send limbs flying here and there, toes stretched, hands careening.

The dance comes from the inside, pushed out with every beat, with every count of choreographed lifts, cracks, and pulls. Chest full of air, head flung back, back arched, palms towards the sky.

13

Connections

She seems focused on something behind me, intense, and her voice reaches me as if carried from far away: you know the world is so huge I cannot comprehend that one is not endlessly in awe of it, endlessly amazed at all possible permutations working themselves out, at all these alternate worlds continuously relegated to mere phantasms.

If we start with ourselves, one human being, and extrapolate to a hundred others, people one knows and loves and has shared time with, scattered all over this planet, and then to the thousands that one will encounter, who will intervene in the course of one's life, in a way which we are still under the illusion we can judge to be beneficial or not - and then other thousands, those we saw, smiled at, observed, overheard, smelled as they passed by, in whose life we were ourselves a fleeting appearance. We can extrapolate from these innumerable people who are somehow connected to us to a million, to those we share a city with, then other countless millions, and so on, until we reach the ceaselessly fluctuating number of souls on this vast earth.

Then imagine that all these people who were for a moment reduced to the insignificant role they have played in your life, are themselves, just like you, the centre of action, belief and meaning. All of these creatures with which you inevitably interact can extrapolate from their own consciousness to a web of interrelated beings, all bound together by ties of thought, emotion, and action. When you make each of these countless others just as much the centre of the world as you are for yourself, then you start to catch a glimpse of the true complexity of the web of which we are all small parts, jewels in Indra's net...

14

Seashore

Do you *see*? She asks, eyes on fire, her smile taking over her face, her forehead ablaze with the sun now sinking fast, projecting a myriad golden particles onto the surface of the rippling waves, Midas shaking them out of his doomed hand. These sparkling reflections shining in the evening light form a blazing strip narrowing at the horizon, a royal path spread out before me, beckoning.

And abruptly, finally, it shifts inside. I see through her eyes, every single gold sparkle, shimmering, twisting, the sun's glory in rippling flakes. My eyes bound out across the water, they fly over the gold landing strip, beacons of sparkles guiding me to an invisible vanishing point, flying towards a waiting future. Thrown out of myself, I disintegrate into these particles, my body, torn, scattered, my blood and veins and breath nothing but ephemeral shining reflections over the ocean, decomposed into ever-shifting patterns of gold.

No longer I, no longer whole, I become her body, her shining eyes, her entranced smile. I am water, air, my skin discrete grains of sand in shifting heaps, my pores rocks and the shells of crabs, the swoosh of shore waves, the thinning air in the emptiness of the sky.

I am the sound of children's babble, the lullabies of mothers and the naked whispers of men.

15
Brasserie

Just at this very moment, she says, as I stare beyond the foam in your beer in the late afternoon sun, I catch the waitress run into the waiter's arms, so glad to see him, enveloping herself in his generous laugh, their conspiratorial, private joy drawing in everything around them, telling the world brashly of their friendship and love and delight in holding one another in this moment.

Through them I see everything in the brasserie with a golden sheen, life again almost unbearably beautiful, rich, abundant, overflowing, outpouring, as if some reckless angel had pushed reality's contrast button all the way up, colours ripening, the play of light revealing the shining of things, sounds ringing distinctly, motion slowed into arcs, forms cast densely.

Then I look at you, into those radiant eyes answering me, framed by the creases and folds of your face that have also become my own, and I know that the suffusing warmth of the glow that binds this couple together also binds us, that those colours are yours as well as mine, and that those particles of gold strewn onto the world's surface came from your outstretched hand.

16

Downriver

She smiles as she bends over the restaurant table, and her eyes shine in the ruby red wine, capturing the sun which shimmers on its surface, ghostly crystal arcs reflected where the glass curves.

This spring river, cascading past terraced fields, she murmurs - focus on one point on the surface and your gaze is carried away in its froth and gurgle, past the smooth stone, splashing against rock, then airborne - shining pearls in the light - and caught up in its gliding path again, turbulent, winding itself out of sight.

Every moment in your life is such a drop, capricious, carried by the flow of time, unforgiving, leading you past pangs of the heart and wide elation, a chance encounter and a last wave, faces in the mirror soon lost forever. Like this drop, you pass stations on a one-way journey, childhood games at dusk, the enchantment of Christmas presents, that endlessly rehearsed first kiss, times that sear your memory. In all of this you are carried, inexorably, cradled, every moment experienced only once.

The stream is always the same, she continues, eyes dreamy - every drop instantly replaced by another, their singularity lost in a continuous flow - the river harmonious, constant, its weight soothing. The river itself structures the memory of people, remains witness to their passing.

When your eye embraces this wider perspective, you realise that these drops are but elements of a stronger flow, that all these joys and games and kisses, harsh words and fights and tears are recurring elements of an unchanging whole, each single event endlessly changing and endlessly the same.

Everything changes, vanishes, is lost forever - but also endures, eternally.

17

Surrender

I remember, she smiles, as you were leaning forward ever so slightly, closing the remaining distance between us, involving me, conspiratorially, into your game, mouthing words with those lips that draw breath and cast spells with equal ease, my gaze on their deliberate articulate movement, those fleshy folds giving birth to syllables that ring replete with their own fullness, that sing their own existence, buttress words which, aligned and strung in shards of sentences, speak of worlds that you have built from the sharpness of a winter morning when the empty city is at your command, from the shapes of shadows lingering on the glistening pavement, from recalling at that very moment a time when you had felt the same exultation of belonging right here, those feelings visiting you again now, as your voice, enchanted, blessed, finds its way into me, conjures up demons too loosely chained, horsemen with steppes to conquer bristling at the gate, and I feel myself falling forward into these images floating between us, opening up as I fall, surrendering all at once all that I protect so efficiently, longing only to taste in the smooth texture of these lips the lingering shreds of that morning mist, of those shadows gliding along the pavement, the expanding feeling in the chest that the city, now, is totally mine.

18

Traces

That lingering smell of someone who just waltzed past, their perfume still hanging in the air, a mixture of wool scarves and the aroma of rain and body warmth, inviting us to fill the vacuum created by their passing, this feeling that they have just been here, this space occupied by their flesh, now vacated for us.

Their presence is still so close you are privy to it, accomplice, but if you let the feeling sink in a little longer it reveals earlier occupants, an unending chain of predecessors who sat on that chair in this café, who slept in the room we stayed in last night, who roamed these passages lost in thought as you are now, who could not even have dreamt of our being here, now, in their shoes.

Do you think they have all moved on, on their way; or do you imagine them as curious ghosts lingering in their cherished haunts, returning to places that now exist only in their fleeting memories, ephemeral multitudes no longer rivaling each other for space, all present in this now we so naively claim to be exclusively ours?

We are chess pieces on a vast board, she concludes, moving in set patterns to fill each other's positions, engaged in variations on proven structures, fulfilling each other's destinies.

19

Reflections

We walk through skyscraper canyons on a gloriously bright day when the sky is vast and endless and thoughts race forever upward. Held in a throng of bodies, cushioned by noise and smells, she looks sideways, focused, intently - then turns to me slowly. Her faraway eyes betray that her mind has been floating among wisps of hot air.

We carry with us untold friendly ghosts, she says, our image held by the smoothness of glass and metal and in the ripples of ponds, our selves multiplied many times over, projected onto all plane surfaces. This family of fragmented, disjointed ephemeral selves always travels alongside us, loyal lieutenants trailing to the left and right, scouting ahead or guarding the rear, shoulder to shoulder.

How often then is it not we who are seen, glimpsed and admired from afar, the object of some anonymous desire lost in the crowd, but one of our reflections, gazed at from the safety of an indirect stare, captured as a dream image until the moment we turn the corner, and our projected self vanishes to reappear on the other side?

How often have we not ourselves engaged these friendly ghosts, as delectable voyeurs privy to a private performance, how often have we not engaged these shadowy partners in our play, in our lives, in our world?

20

Ballroom

Do you remember the tables set for dinner in that cavernous restaurant, she asks, empty glasses flanking symmetrical arrangements of plates, red velour chairs standing guard, the chandelier drooping from the ceiling? The mechanical, rehearsed movements of a lethargic waitress cruelly sentenced to a life of wandering these corridors.

Then your song comes up, the first bars reawakening Cinderella memories, the melody dragging up buried slices of time, that trip speeding on endless highways lost in life and thought, that summer evening dancing with all the windows open, that early morning staring out of the train with the headphones on. Space opens up around you, vistas to explore, from deep inside your stomach this ball of air rises up to fill your chest and escapes your lips in a sigh that sucks in the world.

And then the snare drum kicks in the chorus, all these newly awakened scenes swirling into the maelstrom of the now, the pumping bass quickening the blood, temples pulsating, reservoirs of longing and desire unshackled and released.

Then all at once this desolate ballroom itself comes alive, the crystal fills with wine, chatter and entreaties and unspoken longings rise above steaming plates of venison and trout punctuated by the irregular clatter of silverware on china, laughter rings out against the large mirrors, the repeated chorus casting this gluttonous scene and its irreverent actors to its whimsical lyrics.

21

Whirling

Do you remember, she beams, when we ran onto the wide terrace, the blinding sun reflecting from grey shingle tiles, and swung into spin, right arm pointing at the sky, left arm reaching for the ground, connecting heaven and earth?

The panorama gently blurs as we quicken the pace, trees become shadow signposts flashing by - accelerating, we stretch ourselves into the horizon. At speed, our heads thrown back, shoulders cradled by invisible arms, the chest fills itself into a vast expanse, and the heart swells.

Then we coast, the shadows of our circling bodies casting fluid shapes on the stone. The mind takes leave of its senses, and enters a state of repose, the centre of movement itself unmoved, at rest. An inner space opens up and expands, projected outwards, to embrace the fields behind the terrace, the woods behind the fields, the empty azure sky beyond the woods.

Pushed out of ourselves, we are most present, centred in our rightful place, claiming this air and this light and this sunshine and the swish in our ears. This here and now is also that of our earlier whirling, our soul remembering itself as our bodies spun on glorious mornings in the vast empty grounds of the Shinto shrine, on the deck of that homebound ship, in the circular gallery of that grand museum.

Is this centre then not the centre of the world itself, is this place then not all places, is this time then not all time?

22

Mirrors

Have you ever thought about all the paths not taken, she asks, looked back at the vanishing shapes of irreversible decisions, fate and desire conspiring to mould your choices? For every you that turned right to reflect the golden smile of that Japanese child, another you turned left and walked in the long shadows of the riverbank, the air thick with longing.

We have all split innumerable times, become armies of lookalikes pursuing fractionally different destinies, bountiful families of kindred spirits, forever tied to a common stem. Twin brothers who share our our looks and personalities have pursued variations on the same dream. Our cousins have emigrated to other lives, fallen in love with someone we would not have noticed, forged other blood bonds. Distant relatives with the same childhood memories have scattered further still, found their purpose in lives that leave us indifferent, joined sides we have always opposed, and pray to other gods. Those on the far reaches share only our birth time, but have mutated so far away from us to become altogether other, to become all that we are not, beyond what we can imagine.

And yet how often do we not encounter those mirror selves, are we struck to see the parent with that child that would have been ours, read sentences we would have written, heard snippets of conversation that also came to our mind? Is every other that wears clothes we like, that elicits our warm sympathy for the strength of their ideals, that seduces us with their mischievous smile, not really just our own mirror image made flesh? Every one of our contemporaries is but a version of us, our illusion of uniqueness a thin veil to shelter our fragile identity. In the foolhardy impetuousness of our younger cousins, we recognise the rebel that still lives in us, and every one of our expressions is carving lines on our face, to match those of older friends.

Who are we not? Have we not had it both ways all of the time, have we not all loved and lost and hated versions of our selves, have we not wandered deserts while never leaving home, practiced all possible trades, said all possible things in all living languages, both question and answer, light and shadow, night and day?

And engaged in hand-to-hand combat, in the frenzy and madness of battle, as we sink the blade into our enemy's heart, do we not see in those dying eyes our own mirror self who turned left on that day by the riverbank, now looking straight at us?

23

Boardroom

Do you remember sitting across from me that afternoon in that luxurious office, a dozen of us around that enormous boardroom table, an extensive variety of coffee paraphernalia jostling for space with thick reports and notepads full of doodles, bathed in the bleached glow of fluorescent lights? What *were* you thinking when I caught your eye, where had your roaming mind gone, what strange paths were you travelling on?

The glint of your eye tells me you are not with us, not here among the graphs and strategies and weighty words, but that you are otherwise engaged, tracking disparate ideas in your own wilderness, formulating elusive alliances, taking stock, immersed in your own fairy wonderworld. Or are you already in fantasyland, losing yourself in the long dark hair of the woman across from you, slowly running your hands through it, feeling the tips drag across your cheeks, breathing its perfume body warmth? Are you already focusing on that ear, following its curves, catching the fair down in the sharp light, your fingertips tingling at the ready, your mouth rehearsing nibbling that shapely lobe? Are you fixated on the slow-motion dance of her lips when she speaks, the dark red framing her glistening teeth?

Do you think any of us were really there among graphs and resolutions, in our suits and stockings, silk shirts and power ties, the adrenaline elite of this toy world? Were we not each in our own film, on our private quest, plotting secret coups, rehearsing coming encounters, languorously reliving those last caresses, imagining the laugh of our child when we come home? Were we not a dozen hearts with myriad dreams and untold longings, a dozen minds spinning the contours of the real, bursting with life inside our chests, aching desire set loose?

24

Perfect Day

Do you remember, she asks, you and I hand in hand at the zoo – the heat and the sunlight that licks the shimmering concrete, its glare overflowing speckled rough patches, beating back the shadows into far corners, the foliage above our heads exploding into a hallucinating mosaic of interlaced leaves at our feet, its shamelessly luxurious green vibrant, pulsating, alive with the sharp pitch of unseen birds of dubious origin and untraceable pedigree, a cacophony of calls, warnings, seductions, bursts of proud song replete with missed cues, provoking the distant insulted screeching of chimpanzees.

Can you still smell that heavy bouquet of assorted droppings, wheelbarrows of elephant, zebra, giraffe and okapi dung, the sweet and heavy pregnant stench of the reptile cages, the fragrant manes of sun-drenched lions in basking somnolence, the pungent insistence of the vultures and flamingos, and floating above it all the odour of heat itself, the glorious stink of flesh and sun?

And amidst this bursting animal opulence, strolling through this Fallen Garden, all I sense is the trickle of sweat running between our palms, the feel of your skin glued to mine, in our regal passage through the ones we have chosen for our Ark.

25

Slow song

Where are you? she asks, my mind floating away as this song comes on. I am fifteen again, at our school party, going up to the most beautiful girl in my class to ask her to dance this slow song, to let herself be held, close to me, her chest pressed ever so slightly against me, feeling her arms around my shoulders. Doubts and insecurity overcome, the voice that asks and the ears that hear "yes", it's that moment when she presses herself a little closer, her steps aligned with mine, it's the smell of her skin and the perfume from her mother's cabinet, a dab of her insecurity to match mine. How tentative and fragile it seems now, but how it filled my world then. We do so many things for the first time, stammer and smile, avoid only to yield - and yet as we do this, we replay the songs of the ages, repeat the measured gestures of our courtly grandfathers and the barn dances of forgotten times.

Where now is that tenderness and fear, the feeling that the fate of my world hangs on the yes coming from those lips, where is the tentativeness of the embrace in which we held each other? Everything has moved on, river after river having passed under this bridge – the teenagers we were have become protective mothers and managers tinged with grey. We have inherited the serious world faster than we should have cared for.

That dance, those arms on my shoulders, those fears engaged, and for a moment, that feeling of being at the centre of it all, of everything falling into place, of belonging together within that song, all of that still lingers somewhere. The dance of those atoms, some mine, some hers, that area of space-time of our close dancing remains, held, even if just in our memories. Does everything that once happened, that was once of the utmost importance, not endure somewhere, exist for all eternity? Is not every instant of the present backed up by endless echoes, stretching as far back as memory serves, and farther still? Does that slow dance still exist as surely as my recalling it now, was that dance not danced by the two of us for all eternity?

26

Intermezzo

Do you remember, she asks, that dreary afternoon in the university church, the pompous drone of the speaker, flat analyses drowning in self-importance, the dusk of late afternoon starting to weigh on our hearts, our minds blank, the congregation collectively sinking into drivel? The gaze seeks to lose itself in the nooks and crannies of the arched ceiling, following ancient pathways where dulled gazes have stared for centuries, plotted many an escape, and harboured secret plans, composed love letters, philosophical tracts, and alchemical formulae.

Then at the interval the tall cellist comes on, takes possession of the stage with composed movements - for a moment she remains with her arm suspended, head tilted, brow furrowed, at the ready - and then the first few notes of a Bach sonata are set free from the strings, released into space, where they dance upwards, skirt wooden panels, contour pillars, ricochet against stained glass, and descend again into the fray of the melody. Phrases salute each other without ever touching, like phantom dancers they waltz, notes mirroring each other across invisible timelines, an unseen geometrical pattern becoming sound.

The mind is suddenly reawakened, pursues these notes as they rise higher and higher to the ceiling, every layer another variation, inversion, or counterpoint. Time folded up and replayed, our past self encountering the present, anticipating notes to come. Echoes of the previous motif wash over the current one, notes ripples returning from the end of a pond meeting those still going outward, their layers seamlessly gliding over each other.

Up in those nooks and crannies, these notes find memories of earlier sonatas, they revive long forgotten echoes of cantatas, fugues, plainsong, all the music that this church has sheltered. The cello pays tribute to ghostly performances that came before it, as it revives those notes, born of human minds to soothe human hearts. This space, in which I turn to look at you, now, loses itself in the fullness of time stretched across minutes, hours, centuries.

27

Exile

The world is really just what it is. A stone is a stone, a late afternoon is a late afternoon, and the paved tree-lined streets along the canals are just that. Even the poet tells us that a rose is a rose is a rose. The world is reassuringly solid and enduring, unfolding according to its own physical laws and destiny. The scene that awaits us in the morning on our doorstep is the one we left there the evening before.

It is easy to believe this, and comforting as well. Nothing more than common sense. But it is also plain wrong: the world as we experience it is simply not what it is.

The world we live in, whatever the state of the clouds and the trees, is at times colourless, insipid, a melancholic purgatory in which we are only doing time. Surfaces are painted with a matte finish; sounds are dull and muffled. Gravity not only keeps everything in place but seems to pull things down even further: our conversation feels as heavy as our limbs. For another poet, this was the wasteland.

At other times, light shines out of the things themselves, and the interplay of hues on the texture of objects makes them disturbingly alive. Everything seems to hang in mid-air, no longer harnessed to the ground, and permanently in danger of floating off. Our spirit too is buoyed, light, rising upon thermals.

At those times the world itself has found a beat to drive our hearts. Our steps align themselves with its pace, in synch with its unfolding. There are unheard melodies in the sequences of our impressions, encounters which feel as sonatas, mornings lived as overtures of unfinished symphonies.

How can the very same world feel so different? How can the stone in the late afternoon light radiate the ochre warmth of belonging one day, and mutely reflect dejection and hopelessness the day after? When will the drums pick up again to push us forward, to punctuate our every "yes"? Why do we allow ourselves to fall back, through what mechanism are we exiled from our rightful home?

The Ancient Greeks feared exile more than death. Exile was death within life, it meant feeling the heat of the afternoon without enjoying its warmth, seeing the dappled shadow of the leaves on the earth without being entranced by its pattern, it meant hearing all music as echoes of longing. For the exile, the body survives while the soul withers.

I will inscribe the shining of things, the heartbeat of time and the effervescence of life into my mind with wounds of flesh so deep that just by touching their scars I can remind myself of the ever-present glory of this world, even in those darkest hours of exile.

28

Perpetuum Immobile

It was one of those mornings when I was pacing the room, a caged tiger, caffeine quickening synapses, nerves herding my stray thoughts together, mouthing the opening lines of a speech, tossing one of your juggling balls in the air. The feel of the soft leather leaving my hand, looking up, catching it effortlessly as it falls back into my palm, the dull thud welcome and reassuring. Again and again, I let the ball go, following its trajectory, anticipating its course, my hand reaching out all by itself to meet it in mid-air, two opposite movements wed in that soft touchdown.

Soon I am beneath it, throwing it higher, watching the three-coloured ball swirl upward, diminishing, then coming back at me with patient inexorability. I become part of that rhythm, my body itself reaching up to push it higher, arching my toes, sending it off with the love and care of a proud mother, wishing it up on its ascent, at full stretch when it reaches the top. Then I am making ready for its return, my weight on my heels, watching it come towards me with all the trust and eagerness of a young pup, always finding my hand, demanding the soft squeeze of my fingers. It's up, flight, fall, reach, thud, then up, go, come, catch, thud. My eyes and arm follow this wave, my mouth is open, my mind blank.

And in every throw there is a moment when that glorious ball has spent its climb, just before gravity traps it back towards my hand, a single moment in time and out of time, an instant which does not endure, a slice of life so thin that it cannot be seen, cannot be caught, cannot even be measured, when your juggling ball is neither climbing nor falling but hangs still in mid-air, and my body and this room and this city and this earth freeze with it to achieve a perfect state of rest.

29
Shadows

Do your remember that night, she asks, when we were sitting on the stone steps of the hill, having come out of the church of the Sacred Heart, as the City of Lights stretches before us, speckling the warm air with stars? In the distance, tall towers draw the eye to their luminous beacons, while parks form bald patches in a sea of luminescence covering the slopes. Grand avenues, red and white veins, now coursing around city blocks, now standing still, choreographed by a mosaic of red and green traffic signals. At the bottom of the hill, floodlit corner stores disgorge fruits and vegetables in green, purple, and yellow.

From the foot of the stairs a wave of people undulates upwards, comes closer, and passes us on both sides – we form an island that splits the current. The hill is steep: while children jump with spring step, others measure their pace, turning around to marvel at the view. Camera flashlights reveal impromptu tableaux of generational and romantic groupings. The loose summer clothes on display look very much alike, but a Babelian cacophony of languages reveals that the whole world has gathered here tonight.

In this midsummer languor, movement, conversation, and laughter unfold at ease. Then time speeds up, accelerates, turning our view into fluid time-lapse photography. Waves of visitors, no longer the hundreds that were climbing the hill tonight, the thousands that have come today, or even the millions who have passed through this year, wash over us, still sitting, bemused, on our island. Stretching back in time, smartly-dressed tourists, colourful hippies with long hair, gentlemen shinning with brilliantine, top hats and long skirts, in turn, pass us by. Then the illusion fades, as suddenly as it began.

We realise that every movement made tonight, every gasp and sigh, every word of wonder or surprise, is a reprisal of a scene which has already taken place here, a repetition of a repetition. All this joy and love and amazement, all this sadness and longing and misery, have also been felt, on this hill, by those who came before us. And everything we have done and said tonight will be repeated countless times after us, by the children of our children, by those whose lives are unimaginable to us today. Even with our warm breath so close to each other, blood pumping through our hearts, we are nothing but ghosts, already shadows of time's inexorability.

30

Instant

Do you remember? she asks, cycling along canals in late summer heat, the air tingling with reflected light, the pavement colonised by rosé wine and laughter, windows thrown wide open to the world.

Passing the bridge, looking to my right, I catch a glimpse of a skirt disappearing into a doorway. A green skirt, billowing slightly, two calves walking away, the door about to close. Then we have moved on, cyclists to our left, a car up ahead, an elaborate ballet of wheels, outstretched arms and ringing chimes.

Who is she? Who is the woman with the green skirt who enters the canal house at that moment? Is she coming home, relieved after a day's work, elated because of the sun? Is there someone waiting for her, is she expected, longed for, desired? Or is she coming back to her solitude, mentally rehearsing her plans for the evening, already, in her mind, sinking into a fragrant bath?

What if the wheels of time had moved but slightly differently, if we had pedalled a little faster, reaching her house as she was taking out her keys? Would she have turned to us, would I have caught, for a moment, her expression? Would we, in that instant, have faced each other, and with the recognition one sees in the other's eye, acknowledged each other?

If instead we had lingered a few seconds longer at the red light, I would have seen only a closed door, one among the countless handsome doors lining these canals, anonymously protective of lives inside. My perception of a door closing would not have occurred, nor would this cascade of thoughts have followed. My mind would not have stored that image of a green skirt, ever so slightly raised by the breeze or by the draft, would not have been struck by the movement of the muscle in those calves, turning away.

Every experience in our lives is thus an instant between two realities that did not come to pass, between a moment too soon and a moment just past. The meaning of the images we glimpse eludes us, even on sunny days - they are given to us only as fragments, as pieces of a puzzle, as unanswered questions. Every skirt glimpsed in a open doorway is also a time of missed encounters, of identities not shared, of recognition left wanting.

31

Clouds

After the rumble on the runway, engines throttled, body pushed back against the seat, the plane suddenly floats, arched up, in the air, and the geometric layout of the airport recedes in the mist. Within instants we are enveloped in clouds, and the world outside is cotton balls and puffs, layer upon layer of grey. Then just as suddenly the plane breaks through the clouds: a vast expanse of blue set alight by the sun, more gloriously blue than the earthbound soul can remember. Icarus-like, we climb higher and higher into this azure blue, a shiny sea of white rolling beneath us, so sharp it hurts the eye.

Now that we have levelled off at cruising altitude, our body regains its horizontal, and the plane speeds forward effortlessly in the rarefied air, midway between the heavens and cares left on earth. For the next two hours we pierce blazing blue before us and mark the sky with vapour trails. Up here, there is nothing but space for our thoughts to float upward, buoyed by low cabin pressure and sparkles on every surface. Everything rests in the low hum of the engines, in reverie brought about by the rehearsed and efficient movements of the cabin crew.

Down there, completely out of sight beneath the vast expanse of white cloud, is the world: fields and rivers with roads and train lines streaking through, toy cars speeding back and forth, and countless square buildings. Down there is the grey world of computer screens and fluorescent meetings, of plastic coffee breaks and polite chit-chat, of feelings left unspoken. Below the clouds lie clock time and deadlines, rendezvous and project plans – changing traffic lights in a light drizzle, a builder balancing on scaffolding, the cleaver of the butcher about to chop. There lie dreams and hope, pangs of envy and jealousy, everyday sadness and the savageness of despair.

With the coffee cleared away and tray tables stowed, we are about to forfeit our angel wings. Already our lilt forward signals decent, and that once so-distant white sea is gradually filling our horizon. For one final moment we bask in blue light, then it is a soft imperceptible dive into white. Layer upon layer of grey, puffs and cotton balls, and then the world reappears, lines of cars streaking across fields, the airport runway already to our right. Within moments wheels are on the ground, jets reversed, brakes on, and we are taxiing to the gate.

In the grey world again, through passport controls and custom checks, waiting for our luggage, switching on our phones for incoming messages and upcoming meetings, will we remember to look up now and then? Will we gaze at those layers of grey and recall that far above, an everlasting sun is shining over an impossibly vast stretch of nothing but blue?

32

Levity

Some days are just light. Light as opposed to heavy, with touches of the carefree, a gentle frivolity, time fluid and suspended, a play of possibilities. The discovery of a new song by an old favourite, with a happy melody and ironic lyrics, a song on repeat that burrows its way into my consciousness.

While cleaning out a drawer I throw an old passport in the air, and while I watch it open and spin on the way up, briefly suspended in mid-air before it falls back into my waiting hands, that movement encapsulates the pleasure I had as a child in throwing and catching things, especially bottles as their long necks jerk them in uneven circles upwards, then magically nudge themselves into my open palm when I catch them, it works every time, and while my old blue passport is almost at the top of its flight, in its brief and doomed escape from gravity, I think about the precious stamps on its pages, visible in the briefest of flashes, and the voyages they made possible, the years as a legal guest on a different continent, the status and shelter they provided, and I realise those years are gone forever now, have flowed down time's river along with the rest of the world, while during this washing away of time this old favourite has been writing his songs, clever and playful variations on earlier melodies that enchanted me decades ago, growing older and greyer at the same rate as I have, and I smile at the innocence of a handwritten passport, from a time before scans and memory chips and digital profiling, when states relied on fierce-looking, page-sized multicolour stamps to imprint their authority on documents and minds, and in the lightness of this day, to the tune of this song, all of this looks lovable and quaint.

And I realise that I have never really understood what could be unbearable about the lightness of being, when this lightness and the fount of memories it sends out in sparks is what turns the most mundane of activities on such an ordinary late autumn Tuesday into a miniature celebration of the joy of songwriters and their melodies, of criss-crossing oceans, of meetings and parting, of time savoured and spent, fully, gloriously.

33

I Am Legion

I was being carried with the flow of passengers towards the escalator on the train platform, when I suddenly thought I recognized someone. There he was: tall, slightly gawky, with a full head of curly brown hair, and an expression alternating between mild puzzlement and impish arrogance. I was staring straight into his face, trying to recall where I had seen him before, where we would have met, in which slice of my life this young man had played a part. I was already descending, carried along with the crowd, his face moving out of my field of vision, when it finally hit me.

Making my way through the underground station, trying to get my bearings, I begin to realise whom I just saw: this is the fourteen-year old me, with those curls, that look, that demeanour and that attitude. Even his clothes looked like the kind of thing I used to wear. This is a perfect image of me in the early 1980s, and I must have stood on that very same platform, catching the same train to the North several times that year, now thirty years ago.

Walking down the main hall, I remember a friend of mine who discovered years ago that he had an alter ego, another self, somewhere in the world. That person was the same age, had done the same studies and followed a similar path in life, looked somewhat like him and, most uncannily, had a personality very much like his own. I remember the sense of wonder and reverence with which he explained all this to me, and which cut short the many facile jokes that sprung up in my mind. Over the years, I have sometimes wondered if there was also another I out there, with a similar life history, with my appearance and my character traits. I admit I would not be completely surprised if someone were to tell me that they had met another version of me somewhere.

Coming out onto the plaza now, into the bright sunshine on this cold Spring day, I am starting to realise what it means to have met myself across a thirty-year gap. We do not just have one or more alter egos pursuing their life - which is also partly our life - simultaneously with our own. This would already be a mystery, since the laws of probability allow for so many mutations that similar individuals, except perhaps for twins, should be an extremely rare occurrence.

The real situation, I begin to fear, is far worse, phantasmagorical, the stuff of shifting realities and uneasy dreams. We do not only have alter egos living in our own time, somewhere mercifully far away, whom we are unlikely to run into. We also have, strewn across the world but also across slices of time, our own selves at different ages. How many of these other selves exist out there, now breathing the air we breathed five, ten, or thirty years ago, walking with the same gait, laughing the same laugh, having, for all we know, similar thoughts to those we had then?

Now that I am beginning to understand, motionless on the Plaza by the taxi stand, now that the fog is lifting, I suddenly recall an earlier encounter, a few years back. I was irritated by a noisy, hyperactive child when I realised I was exactly like that in my youth. It felt then, already, that I was looking at a former self, although not with the intensity of the face that I saw today, which was my face.

As I slowly start to walk into the city, I am becoming calmer, now that the truth is out. I wonder how many more other selves I will meet, how close the circles are that we move in, how likely a new encounter will be. A wave of feeling washes over me, a deep sense of love for those other selves, for all those who are now living the life that is also mine. It seems trite, and not completely accurate, to think of us as connected. In reality, the threads that link us are slender at best, as if it was planned that we should pass each other by at a distance. We are far more than related, we are mirror images of each other, we are each other.

Waiting at a traffic light, looking at the shiny reflection of the sun in the water, I suddenly think of another possibility. Will I, by chance, only run into younger other selves, or is there an alter ego somewhere out there that has already lived longer than I have, the extra years etched into a face that will be mine to turn into? Will I even be able to recognize a face that I have not yet become, an alter ego from an unlived future?

34

Survivor's Pride

As you walk towards me, I notice that you have brought your parents today. Your father on your right, his characteristic gait mirrored in the decisive steps you take, your mother on your left, her bright curiosity lighting up your eyes as well. They seem particularly happy, as they haven't come alone. Behind them, your grandparents, a lot younger than I remember them, are chatting away. Behind them, a little fainter in this bright air, some smartly dressed people who must be their parents - the great-grandparents you never knew, all eight of them. They are in turn flanked by their parents, who look upon them as proudly as your parents look upon you.

You are quite a sight this morning, walking at the apex of a pyramid of ancestors that stretches back as far as I can see, a veritable army of your kin, and I realise that this throng behind your shoulders have all passed into you, through their blood, their genes, their stories of loss and victory, their love of life and for each other. Small parts of them reside in you, have survived centuries of turmoil and chance, have mutated into your very flesh and bones. You, like all of us alive today, are the ultimate survivor in the game of life, you are the finest that has been produced, you beat out all the other possible you's that did not come into existence. You stretch back as far into time as the crowd behind you, and I had never fully realised how composite you really are.

In front of you, your two children are skipping, restless as always. They too seem particularly proud today, with all their family in tow. When I focus on their faces, yours seems to recede somewhat, and I imagine that one day, when they will have become the man and woman you so hope they will become, the elements of your face that I have seen grow into adulthood will be carried by them, split between them, carried forward with the same survivor's pride I can make out in you today.

35

The Last One Before the Final One

Do you remember the waiter bringing our first two glasses of beer, she asks, golden in early Spring sunshine, after we had run into each other by accident, coincidence, serendipity, and forsaken all the obligations of an afternoon pledged to weighty things? Catching up after all these months, waterfalls of tales, how fitting it all is, how it reaffirms you and me and what we do and the world and all its mad business.

We are having one more, thirst awakened, and I become engrossed in your story with its rambling plot and twists and turns, its larger-than-life characters, its pain and frustration and elation and salvation, marvel at how what happens to you is always so much you, for as long as I have known you. I am caught up again in that part of the world which follows your rules, your face alive with its manifold movements, and we decide we are just going to have one more, and I tell you about the intricacies of what I am going through, my stretched-out fairy tale with its reluctant prince, its mortgaged castle, its inefficient spells. You latch onto my words, make me wonder why I had only seen it in this way, cause my mind to dig deeper, stretch further, and reveal a host of other approaches, sensibilities, interventions.

Then we decide to have a last round, and you speak of the endless pull of all that you want always just being just out of reach, groping for it but never quite catching it. You light up as you speak of your infallible plan to finally get there, and with your loud laugh you exult in the realisation that you and I know that this will, mercifully, never happen. I see in the you I just met again after all these months the you I have always felt existed inside me, feel the pull of those invisible strings tying our hearts together and, looking past the sun on the canals into your eyes, realise that this is the reason we have burned up so much of our life together.

We decide to have one last round, definitely the last one, and we just sit talking loudly and laughing, recounting what happened those times we were together twenty years ago, when you were silly, and I was silly, and Thank God we didn't realise how silly we really were. I understand that in all these months you were not really that far away, that there is so much of you I carry inside, so much of me that has somehow infected you, and we can't help but beckon the waiter to assure him that this one will definitely, absolutely, be the final one.

www.ingramcontent.com/pod-product-compliance
Lightning Source LLC
LaVergne TN
LVHW090125160826
845673LV00015B/1011
9789493375000